Date Due

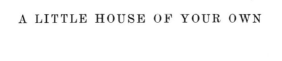

A LITTLE HOUSE OF YOUR OWN

A LITTLE
HOUSE OF
YOUR OWN

by BEATRICE SCHENK DE REGNIERS

Drawings by IRENE HAAS

Harcourt, Brace & World, Inc., New York

TEXT COPYRIGHT 1954 BY BEATRICE SCHENK DE REGNIERS
ILLUSTRATIONS COPYRIGHT 1954 BY IRENE HAAS

N.2.70

LIBRARY OF CONGRESS CATALOG CARD NUMBER : 55-5236
HARDBOUND EDITION ISBN 0-15-245787-9

LIBRARY EDITION ISBN 0-15-245788-7

PRINTED IN THE UNITED STATES OF AMERICA BY
THE MURRAY PRINTING COMPANY, MASSACHUSETTS

To Harry and Sophia Freedman
who set the table
I lived under

WRITTEN IN SECRET MEADOWS AT TUILAUVENT

Everyone has to have a little house
of his own.

Every boy has to have
his own little house.

Every girl should have a little house
all to herself.

Of course you live in a house
with your mother and father.

But that isn't what I mean.
That isn't what I mean at all.

This is what I mean . . .

When I was a little girl
my mother had a dining room table.
It was a round table with a big
white tablecloth on it.

When I was a little girl
I lived under the dining room table.
Not all the time of course. Just
sometimes.

When the grownups were eating supper
I lived under the dining room table
and nobody could see me. Nobody
knew where I was.

I lived under the dining room table
and looked at my picture book, and
under the dining room table was just
like a house for me.

A secret house. Nobody could see me.
Nobody could find me.

Then the grownups would say,
"Where is Beebsie?" "Have you
seen her?" "Now *where* could
that child be?"

And all the time I was in
my secret house
my under-the-table house
my little house all to myself.

There are many kinds of
secret houses. There are
many places where you can have
your own little house.

This is what I mean . . .

When I grew too big to live
under the dining room table
I had another secret house
'way up in a tree.

Nobody could see me
in my secret house in the tree.
When people looked up in the tree
they couldn't see me at all.

All they could see were
the many many leaves. But
I could look down and see
everyone if I wanted to.

I could see my mother
digging in the garden.

I could see my father
lying in the hammock.

I could see the milkman
bringing three quarts of milk.

I could see the dog
scratching fleas.

I could see the cat
chasing a butterfly.

I could see everybody
if I wanted to.

ut nobody could see me
my secret house
in the tree.

Sometimes I took cookies
up to my tree house.

Sometimes I invited a friend
to visit me and have a teaparty
in my tree house.

You can invite a friend
to come to your secret house.
But nobody can come unless
you say so.

I had a friend named
Martha.

Martha had a little house
of her own in the back yard.
Martha's grandfather built it
just for her.

Martha's house had a roof and
windows and a little door. It was
just big enough for two children.

Martha's house had a chimney
on the roof and curtains on
the window and inside the house
were two little chairs
and a table—just right
for Martha and me.

Your own little house doesn't have to
have windows with curtains
or a chimney
or a door.

A big umbrella
makes a fine house.

A secret house just
for you.

A cave behind the bushes
is a good little house.
No one can find you there.

In bed you can have
your own little house
for a little while—
under the blankets.

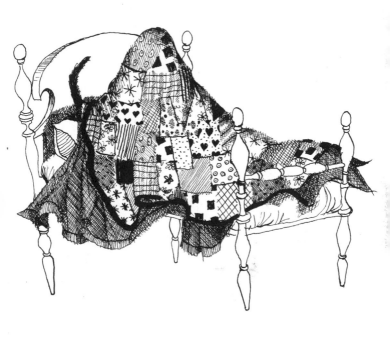

Just you and the pussy cat.

A big box is a good house.

You can jump out and
surprise people.

Of course you don't always
want to be in your own
little house all by yourself.

Not even most of the time.

Just sometimes.

Most of the time
it is fun to be with
other children—

playing tag

or playing catch

or games

or digging in the sand

or eating ice cream
at a birthday party!

And it's fun to be with
grownups —

going to the zoo

or to the store

or listening to a story.

But sometimes you just
want everyone to leave you
alone.

No children.
No grownups.

You just don't want anyone
to bother you.

Then it is a good thing
to have a little house
of your own.

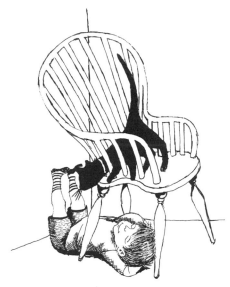

Behind a chair in a corner
can be a good house.

A big hat is like
a little house.

A false face is a
little house for your face.

When you wear a false face
nobody can see your real face.

Your real face
is in a little house
and nobody can see it.

Your papa is in *his*
own little house when
he is behind his newspaper.

He wants everyone to leave him
alone. He doesn't want
anyone to bother him.

No children.
No grownups.

When your mama takes
a nap it is just as though
she has gone into
her own little house and
shut the doors and the windows.

She wants everyone to leave her
alone. She doesn't want anyone to talk
to her or to ask
her questions.

If you tickle her
she will wake up —

and then she won't be
in her own little secret house
anymore.

But that really isn't fair, is it?

Would your mother let you
put an old blanket over two chairs?
That makes a cozy house —

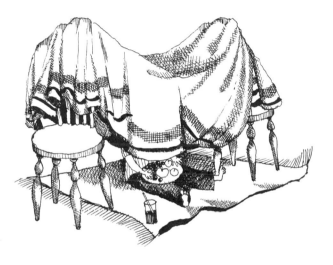

just like a tent.

Do you have a big armchair
in your house? You can
curl up in the seat
just like a pussy cat and
the big armchair will be
a little house for you.

Sometimes
when you sit on your father's lap
and he holds you in his arms
it is just as though you are
in a little house — a little house
just for you.

And when your mother
puts her arms around you
it is just like a little
house — a little house of
your own.

You can find many little
houses. You can make
many little houses just
for you.

And this is the important
thing to remember . . .

Everyone has to have
a little house of his own.

Every boy has to have his own
little house. Every girl
should have a little house
to herself.

And one more thing is
important too . . .

When you are in your own
little house no one should
bother you. Everyone should
leave you alone if you want to
be alone.

If somebody *has* to bother you —
if your mother has to tell you to
get ready for dinner because it is
dinnertime—
then she should be very polite.

She should walk softly
and knock gently at the door
of your little house and she
should speak quietly and tell
you, "Pretty soon it will be time to
leave your little house and get
ready for dinner."

And if *you* should be walking
near somebody's little house
remember

to be very polite

walk softly
speak gently.